Dear Santa

Written by Marcy Kelman
Illustrated by Steve Brown

bookoli

'It's time to write your letter, Lily, for **Santa Claus** to see.

So he knows what treats to leave for you beneath our Christmas tree."

"But will Santa read it?" asks Lily.

"He has so much to **do**!

Making **dolls** and **trains** and **books** and **wrapping** them all up, **too**.

"He must get so **many** letters, asking for presents around the tree.

Will he really

find the time

to read a letter

sent from **me**?"

"It's Christmas **magic**, Lily!
Santa can do it **all**.
But he also has
a **bit** of help
from friends
who are all
quite small...

"Santa's little helpers,
are a magic team of elves.
They work inside the mailroom,
stacking all the shelves.

MAIL ROOM 1

"They bring in bags of letters from children everywhere.

And sort out wishes into piles with lots of giggles and care.

"The elves all have their checklists
for all the girls and boys.
As Santa looks at letters,
elves collect the toys.

Good ☑ Bad ☐

Cookie
Shampoo

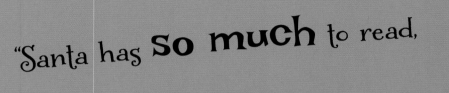

"Santa has **so much** to read,

through lists he speeds and speeds.

Even in the **bathtub**,

he reads and reads

and reads!"

Lily's smile **grows big**,

as she thinks about what to write.

"Oh, I **really** hope Santa visits me on Christmas Eve night!"

Lily starts her letter
with a **sneaky plan** in mind.
She asks for a Christmas gift
that's truly **one-of-a-kind**.

"A **rainbow-glitter skateboard,**
a present like no other!
No one knows I want one,
not my parents or my brother."

Santa, I've been really good,
studying hard at school.
I listen to my parents,
and follow every rule.

I'll leave you a tasty pie
in our blue toy chest.
Merry Christmas, Santa!
You really are the BEST!

Lily

Lily sends the letter,
and then she couldn't **believe**,

How time **raced by** in such a flash
and soon it was **Christmas Eve!**

With a plate filled for **Santa**,
Lily runs up to the chest.
"Hmmm ... maybe I'll give
Christmas magic
another little test."

Lily races to her room,
and finds just the place.
"I'll hide Santa's treats
in a locked suitcase!"

After secretly hiding the key, Lily clambers into bed.
"Tomorrow I will know if my letter was really read."

Early on Christmas morning,
Lily races down the stairs.
Presents, how exciting!
Books and **toys** and **bears**.

Then Lily takes a look around.
Where could the skateboard **be**?
"I guess I was right all along.
No skateboard for me."

As she puts away her toys,
she notices something **shiny**.
A **rainbow-glitter helmet**
with a note that is quite tiny.

It reads: 'Thank you, Lily, for my Christmas treat.

Though it was hard to find, it was truly delicious to eat.'

Racing to her room
with a smile on her face,
Lily finds the skateboard
in the locked suitcase.

Santa read her letter!
He left another note for her too:
'A little Christmas magic is my real gift to you!'